SKY CLOUD CITY

This book belongs to

Dedicated to young readers across the globe.
Dream big and aim for the stars.
The sky is the limit . . .

-M.K. -N.K.

For information about special discounts available for bulk purchases, sales promotions, fund-raising and educational needs, please contact the publisher littlecentaurpress@yahoo.com .

Published by LITTLE CENTAUR PRESS
798 S. Branch Pkwy, Springfield, MA, 01118, USA.
www.littlecentaurpress.com
littlecentaurpress@yahoo.com

First edition July 2021
Paperback ISBN
978-1-7324758-7-8
Library of Congress Control Number
2021934518

TEXT: Maria Kamoulakou-Marangoudakis

ILLUSTRATIONS: Natalia Kapatsoulia

EDITING & PROOFREADING: Robin Katz, Carl Marangoudakis

LAYOUT: Ina Melengoglou — altsys.gr

COVER DESIGN: Natalia Kapatsoulia & Ina Melengoglou

SKY CLOUD CITY

Written by
MARIA KAMOULAKOU

Illustrated by
NATALIA KAPATSOULIA

THE ADVENTURES OF
Hope & Trusty

Chapter One

A CAREFREE CHILDHOOD

Once upon a time in a far-away land across the deep blue sea, there lived two best friends: a girl named Hope and a boy named Trusty.

Hope and Trusty were young, bright, and curious. Like most children their age, they enjoyed exploring the world around them, and their curiosity often got them into trouble.

They lived in a large and busy city named Athens. This city was famous all around the ancient world for its beautiful public buildings made of marble. It was also well-known for its skillful crafters, gifted poets, talented artists, eloquent philosophers, and prominent politicians.

Hope and Trusty were born and raised in a neighbor-hood of little mud-brick houses, at the foot of a steep hill with towering fortifications called the *Acropolis*. In this place, people found refuge in times of war and danger. Within its mighty walls stood the jewel of Athens: the famous temple of their patron goddess Athena, the so-called *Parthenon*.

You see, the people of Athens, including Hope and Trusty, worshipped not one god—but twelve! All twelve gods had human characteristics and were known to be notorious gossipers! They lived in a luxurious palace built on the highest peak of Mount Olympus—a tall mountain always covered with clouds. Yet, they were always turning their attention towards Earth! They loved to interfere in people's lives, and they often descended from Mount Olympus to interact with the people.

These Olympian gods enjoyed gifts, as well as meat offerings roasted over an open fire. The thick smoke that rose from those fires invited the gods to their temples. There, a share of the feast awaited them on the altars.

As children in Athens, how many times did Hope and Trusty chase each other along the winding alleys of their neighborhood?

"Catch me if you can!" Hope giggled, racing down the hill like a gazelle.

How many times did Trusty trip and fall, scraping his knees on these rough dirt roads?

"Oh, no! Not again . . . !" Trusty cried—in anger rather than pain—because he had failed to catch up with Hope once again.

Every now and then, the two friends would race all the way to the *Agora*—a dusty, noisy marketplace. A variety of goods were sold or traded there every day. The Athenian fleet sailed the seas and brought back all sorts of products to the city's merchants: from grain and wheat flour to exotic fabrics, spices, incense, and live animals.

"Fish! Fresh fish! Salted fish! You name it, we have it!" shouted the fisherman—loudly advertising his catch of the day from behind his bench at the marketplace.

"Pots and pans, ladies! Made of good quality clay. Well-baked and sturdy, exactly as you like them!" exclaimed the potter from the entrance of his store.

"Affordable leather shoes for you and your family! Step inside to try the latest fashion!" The shoemaker waved his arms vigorously to a group of young men, inviting them inside his store.

"Or bring your old shoes, if you prefer, to have them mended," he added as they passed by. It was just another typical day in the marketplace!

Chapter Two
LOOK WHO IS TALKING!

One day, Hope and Trusty raced happily to the *Agora* in a cloud of dust. Two stray dogs, Chewy and Lazy, trailed after them, barking all the way.

"Hey, you two! Slow down! Slow down!" yelled a merchant as they entered the courtyard of the *Agora*. Hope and Trusty ran straight for their favorite tree: a tall Platanus with wide branches extending on all sides like an umbrella. They folded their arms around its thick trunk to catch their breath.

"I love you, gentle giant," whispered Hope, gently resting one cheek against the tree's scaly bark. *I love you toooooo . . .* she thought she heard the tree whisper in reply . . .

The two dogs whimpered behind them, begging for attention and a few affectionate strokes on the head. Hope and Trusty were old friends with the dogs, who frequently accompanied them when they were playing.

"Good boy, Chewy. You raced well!" whispered Trusty, tapping the dog on his backside. Lazy brushed against Hope's leg for attention.

Then, suddenly, Chewy turned around! In the blink of an eye, the dog started running towards the pet store across the street, barking loudly at a pair of pitch-black crows.

"No, Chewy, no!" yelled Trusty, running after him. In a flash, Lazy followed them to the entrance of the pet store.

The two crows hopped restlessly from perch to perch in their small cage. With slender black legs, thick black beaks, and lustrous black plumage, the two crows were as dark as the legendary Greek goddess, Nyx, known as the Black-Feathered Night!

Mesmerized by the beauty of the two crows, Hope followed Trusty, and together they approached the cage. The two birds stopped hopping back and forth and sat quietly side-by-side, on the highest perch. As the sun's rays warmed their feathers, they sparkled with a lustrous deep-blue sheen. Each crow elongated its neck and fixed a bright eye on Hope and Trusty. Much to their relief, Chewy had stopped barking and was now wagging his tail while looking at Trusty.

"They are so pretty! Look at their feathers!" Hope said, breaking the silence as she pointed at the birds with her finger.

"I wonder where they came from," replied Trusty, moving his face closer to the cage.

And suddenly . . .

"*Kr-aack, kr-aack.* We come from the Land of the Birds," answered one of the crows.

"Yes, yes! The Land of the Birds," repeated the other crow. To their amusement, Trusty jumped in surprise, and Hope stepped backward, tripping over Trusty's feet and falling over.

"This can't be real!" exclaimed Trusty as he helped Hope back to her feet. "No bird can speak with a human voice!"

"*Kr-aack, kr-aack.* Where we come from, *all* the birds speak with a human voice. Our kingdom is magical," pointed out the other crow, keeping a close eye on the children's reaction. "Free us, and we will take you there," he added with a strange tone in his voice.

At first, the two friends were bewildered. They looked at one another with raised eyebrows and moved away from the cage to talk it over. They counted their pocket money and found it lacking. In the meantime, in anticipation, the crows began to hop back and forth again, like a pendulum.

"I say we do it," declared Trusty in a firm voice. "It is late summer, and our friends have all gone to their country homes. Our parents are busy gathering grapes. It will be a couple of weeks before we can join them in the countryside. Let's have some fun, Hope! Life in the city is so boring in the summer!" he whined.

Hope, who always trusted Trusty's judgment, agreed to his proposed plan without giving it much thought. She had some savings at home. If they put their pocket money together, they should have enough to purchase the birds—and perhaps buy a few provisions for their journey. Trusty approached the cage to introduce himself and Hope to the crows.

"I am Trusty," he said. "And this is my best friend, Hope," he added, taking Hope by the hand. "What are your names?"

"I am Blackie," replied one of the crows.

"And I am Pluckie," added the second crow.

"Can anyone tell you apart?" Hope asked, glancing from one to the other.

"Not really!" Pluckie explained. "People can only tell us apart when I get stressed out, and I pluck a few feathers from my legs . . ."

"Well, Blackie and Pluckie," Trusty interrupted, "we have decided to buy you tomorrow. You will lead us to your magical kingdom—and after that, will we set you free." Blackie and Pluckie cawed with happiness.

"Thank you for your kindness, Hope, and Trusty," Blackie said. Then he spoke again. "The sun has risen and set seven times since the day we were captured. Back in the Land of the Birds, our friends and family must be worried sick."

"You won't regret the trip," Pluckie added. "I promise you that! But be prepared for a long and tiring walk. Bring a hat with you, and some food for the road."

Promising to meet with the crows again the next day, Hope and Trusty waved goodbye to them. The two friends took the long way home, thinking about all the things they had to discuss. They knew they'd have many important plans to make. They could hardly wait for tomorrow!

Chapter Three
OFF TO THE UNKNOWN!

The next morning, Hope and Trusty awoke to the deafening song of the cicadas. The time had come to quietly get away and meet under the Platanus tree in the marketplace. They knew they had better be on the road before the unforgiving summer sun had a chance to rise high in the sky!

As if by magic, the two stray dogs sniffed them out, racing to join them in the marketplace. Hope and Trusty met under the tall Platanus tree. They had each packed a flask of water, some bread, a handful of dried fruit, and some nuts for the journey.

As soon as the pet store opened, they rushed inside, bought the crows, and off they went! "Good morning, friends! Are you ready?" asked Blackie with a wink, as they left the *Agora* behind them.

"Yeaaaaah!!!" Hope and Trusty jumped up and down with joy.

"Off we go, then!" added Pluckie, sticking his beak out of the cage with anticipation.

With loud *kr-aacks* and *caws*, the two crows guided Trusty and Hope out of the city through the towering main gate. Trusty held the cage firmly in his hand for fear of dropping it on the ground. At the gate, Hope gave her best smile as they exited, but the guards were not at all friendly. They frowned at the group with curiosity and suspicion through their bronze helmets.

What a strange sight they were! Two crows in a cage, a boy and a girl, and two stray dogs with their tongues hanging out.

"Keep moving, Hope," whispered Trusty into her ear. "Keep moving before the guards start asking questions."

Their unusual company of two friends, two birds, and two dogs followed a dirt road that led them north. This route steered them away from the cultivated fields and the city dwellers' summer estates.

Blackie and Pluckie decided to keep everyone entertained with bird jokes.

"Have you heard the joke about the broken egg?" asked Pluckie.

"Nooooope!" Hope answered.

"I have," said Blackie, "It cracked me up!"

"Where does a peacock go when it loses its tail?"

"I have no idea," said Trusty, laughing.

"It goes to a re-tail store!"

"I know one!" Hope jumped in, eager to share her joke. "What do you give to a sick bird?"

"Oh, that's an easy one," replied Pluckie. "Tweetment!"

Then Trusty joined in, asking, "How about this one? "What do you call a bird in the winter?"

"Brrrrrr-d!" answered Hope, giggling.

"Here's my favorite one!" interrupted Blackie. "Who is the penguin's favorite Aunt?"

The two friends looked at each other, frowning in bafflement. With a big grin, Blackie looked back at them, happy to reveal the answer:

"Aunt-Arctica!"

At around midday, still laughing and joking, their unusual group of two friends, two birds, and two dogs stopped to rest near a noisy, bubbling creek. They sought shelter in the cool shade of the trees that grew along its banks. Soon after, they unpacked a few nuts for the birds, some bread for the dogs, and a handful of dried fruit for the two friends. It was just what they needed before setting off again.

The city was barely visible on the horizon when the journey became mountainous, and fatigue began to set in. Climbing at a slower and heavier pace, Hope and Trusty made it up the slope. The bushes scraped their bare calves, and thorny seeds got stuck in their sandals.

"Are we nearly there?" Hope whined, wiping the sweat from her forehead with the back of her hand.

"How much longer?" Trusty demanded to know, raising the cage up to his face to communicate his sense of urgency to the birds.

"*Kr-aack, kr-aack.* Not long," responded the crows. "The end of our journey is near. The Land of the Birds lies beyond that summit. There, you will meet our king." It seemed as though the hardest part of their journey was behind them.

Chapter Four
OVER THE SUMMIT

A winding trail led them up

towards a mountain summit covered in fog. Their unusual company of two friends, two birds, and two dogs disappeared in the fog, not knowing what lay ahead. The crows pushed forward with loud *kr-aacks*. Suddenly, just beyond the summit, a gentle breeze moved the fog aside, revealing an entirely new world. A vast valley surrounded by mountain peaks lay before them. A bright, green forest, sparkling streams, and small lakes were visible on the horizon. And of course, there were thousands of birds flying everywhere, as far as the eye could see. There were birds large and small. Some of them boasted bright, colorful plumage, while others wore more muted, dull hues.

As the two friends stood open-mouthed, admiring this new world, the sudden high-pitched cries of the crows startled them.

"*Caw-caw. Caw-caw,*" Blackie and Pluckie cried out as loudly as they could, flapping their wings excitedly in anticipation of freedom.

"*Drrrrrrrrrrr, cha-aa-ah, cha-aa-ah,*" replied a woodpecker from a nearby tree. "Oh, be quiet! Who is calling for my king? What business do you have with him?"

Trusty spoke first, with confidence. "We have traveled a long way to meet your king."

"And to admire his kingdom," Hope added, as she slowly opened the cage door to set the crows free.

The two crows squeezed themselves through the tightly-fitting door. Out of gratitude, they fluttered around Hope's and Trusty's heads several times before landing. Pluckie perched on Hope's shoulder and Blackie on Trusty's. The two friends smiled and gently petted the birds' bellies.

"Our king is taking his afternoon nap after dining on blueberries and locusts. I will wake him up if I must, but he is not going to like this," warned the woodpecker before disappearing behind a nearby thicket.

"*Oop, oop, oop, upupa, upupa!* Who dares disturb my sleep?" cried King Hoopoe in a grumpy mood, as he flew out of a bush. Glaring at the two kids, he continued, "What are you two doing in my kingdom? We are in the Land of the Birds. Don't you know that humans are not allowed here?"

Trusty and Hope bowed their heads respectfully towards King Hoopoe while sneaking a peek at his colorful feathers.

"Your Highness, we have traveled far to visit your kingdom, and we are truly exhausted. With your permission, we would like to rest here for a few days and admire your world before we return to our city," Trusty requested respectfully. He bowed his head even lower while staring at the ground beneath his feet. Then the two crows joined in.

"*Kr-aack, kr-aack!* Greetings, your Highness!" Blackie said. "These two humans helped us escape from the Land of the People."

"We promised they could explore our world in return," added Pluckie. He pleaded, "Please, could they stay with us for a while?"

The king shook his orange head with its tall, fanlike crest. "This is a serious matter, my boys. I cannot decide on my own." He turned to the woodpecker and gave him a royal command. "Wake up my wife, Queen Nightingale, and ask her to summon the birds with her divine singing. *They* will decide what to do with these two."

It wasn't long before the most beautiful melody filled the air. It was the most exquisite music that human ears had ever heard! Trusty and Hope gasped in amazement as Queen Nightingale used her magnificent voice to summon the birds with enchanting notes and playful melodies.

Soon, King Hoopoe joined in with his own song. *His* summoning of the birds extended to the four corners of the Earth. It echoed across valleys, lakes, and streams, reaching over the tallest mountains and across the deep blue sea.

"*Oop, oop, oop, upupa, upupa.* My fellow feathered friends who feed in the sown fields, come forth."

"*Cheer-cheer,*" responded the robins. "We are on our way, Your Highness." And they let the worms live another day.

"*Oop, oop, oop, upupa, upupa.* My friends who bathe in the streams and fly over the tall mountains, come forth."

"*Ki-ki-ki,*" replied the eagles. "We will be there, Our Lord." And they immediately abandoned the snake hunt.

"*Oop, oop, oop, upupa, upupa.* My friends who hunt insects in the marshes, and who chase the waves in the sea, come forth."

"*Chirp-chirp,*" answered the swallows. "We are coming, Our King." And they stopped chasing mosquitoes.

"*Uh-uh,*" responded the seagulls. "We are on our way, Your Eminence." And they gave up fishing for the day.

"*Oop, oop, oop, upupa, upupa.* And you who nest in the woodlands and the bushes, come closer. We have important issues to discuss."

"*Cheer-cheerie-cheer,*" responded the cardinals. "We are at your command, Your Highness." And they flew out of their hiding places. Quite a few birds were already on their way to meet the king, and many more would also be going!

Chapter Five
BIRDS OF A FEATHER

Before long, flapping wings of all sizes covered the sky. Birds were pouring in from all over the world—abandoning fields, forests, rivers, oceans, mountains, and cities, as they answered the call of their king. With great awe and wonder, Trusty and Hope watched birds of all sizes and colors begin to line up on the branches of the surrounding trees.

Hawks, eagles, and owls occupied the tallest branches. Next, the pigeons, sparrows, bluebirds, blue jays and swallows, robins, titmice, chickadees, and cardinals took their places. After that, the roosters, pheasants, peacocks, grouses, and wild hens appeared through the bushes. Blackie and Pluckie perched on a branch above Hope and Trusty. They were all there—including the ducks and the geese, the storks, the pelicans, and the seagulls. Even the swans and the flamingos arrived from far-away lakes, while the parrots came in from distant lands, and the hummingbirds flew in from the tropical forests. All of

27

the birds twittered with excitement and curiosity, eager to find out the reason for this great assembly!

As Trusty and Hope took a good look around them, a sudden chill made their hearts leap. Never before had they seen such a large gathering of birds! They found each other's hands and held on tight. There was good reason to be afraid. Not all of the birds appeared to be friendly . . . In the meantime, the two dogs sensed their friends' fear and started barking.

"Down, Chewy! Sit!" Hope instructed the dog, kneeling to embrace him.

Trusty added, "Shhhh! Hush now, Lazy! Be a good girl and be quiet," while patting Lazy on the head.

"*Oop, oop, oop, upupa, upupa.*" The king's call echoed through the trees of the forest. "My feathered friends, we are all gathered here to decide

whether these two humans—this young man, Trusty, and this young lady, Hope—should be allowed to stay with us in the Land of the Birds." The wild turkey irritably fluffed up his feathers and fanned his tail in anger.

"*Gobble-gobble!*" he shouted. "The idea is outrageous! We cannot allow humans here. They are our worst enemies!"

"*Kr-aack, kr-aack,*" said one crow. "They hunt us down for fun."

"*Quack-quack,*" agreed one of the ducks. "They roast us in the oven with potatoes."

"*Chirp-chirp,*" added one of the swallows. "They kill us and use our feathers to make costumes and hats."

"*Tweet-tweet,*" replied another. "They catch us with large nets and keep us trapped in zoos."

"*Whooh, whooh,*" hooted the owl.

"Humans keep us in tiny cages in their homes and expect us to sing for their amusement. Is that kind of life fit for a bird? I say we should show no mercy to these humans," he insisted.

"*Gobble-gobble!*" the turkey declared. "Come! Birds of a feather flock together! Let's chase them out of our land with our pointed beaks."

Hope and Trusty drew even closer together and trembled in fear. Speechless with fright, they watched the proceedings. They were just about to turn around and flee like rabbits when they heard King Hoopoe address the assembly.

"My friends, please hear me out," said the king. "You all know the twin crows, Blackie and Pluckie. The sun rose and set seven times since they went missing. These kind children, Hope and Trusty, rescued them from the Land of the People and returned them safely home to us. Please give them a chance to speak for themselves."

As King Hoopoe and the two crows tried to hush the assembly, Trusty took a deep breath and stepped forward. At first, his voice quivered, but gradually it grew steadier and louder. Trusty began his speech by explaining that neither he nor his friend Hope had ever harmed a bird in their lives. On the contrary, they had always admired birds for their flying and hunting abilities, bright colors, beautiful singing, and unique elegance.

"My feathered friends," Trusty called out in a steady voice, "I know that we humans have done you wrong, even though you deserve our respect. After all, you have existed on this planet for a much longer time than we humans and our twelve Olympian gods can claim."

During Trusty's speech, Hope was hiding behind his back, occasionally nodding her head, and glancing at the assembly over his shoulder. The birds became silent. Many of them tilted their heads to take a good look at the speaker. Others flew closer to hear the boy more clearly. The truth and wisdom of Trusty's words caught their attention. Encouraged by the birds' silence, Hope cautiously moved closer to Trusty. Now, the two friends stood shoulder-to-shoulder in front of the assembly.

Trusty eagerly continued, "As we all know, at the beginning of Time, there was deep darkness and endless Night. Then, Nyx, the Dark-Feathered Night, laid an egg. And out of it jumped the god of love, Eros, with sparkling golden feathers. In time, Eros laid more eggs and created your race long before the Earth, the sea, and the sky. These events happened long before we humans and our gods came into being." The birds agreed, all nodding at each other and letting out short cries.

Trusty went on, "Let me remind you then, that back in the early days, you used to be kings and rulers of distant and prosperous lands." While speaking, Trusty moved slowly through the assembly. "The rooster became the King of Persia, the cuckoo bird ruled over Egypt and Phoenicia, and the peacock used to be the King of India," he continued, pointing at a colorful peacock in a nearby bush. "Take a good look at him. He walks upright, like a king. He still wears his tall, feathered crown and his royal robe with pride. Have any of you not admired the jewels on his regal robe?"

"Yes! Yes! Very true. Very true," agreed the birds, looking at one another.

With sparkling eyes, Hope watched her friend win over the bird assembly. Seeing his success, she felt less scared while she patiently waited for the right time to jump in and participate. Finding the atmosphere less hostile than before, the two dogs rested peacefully at their friends' feet. Yet, they

were always ready to jump up and defend Trusty and Hope with their sharp teeth.

Feeling more and more confident, Trusty continued, "Even our mighty god, Zeus, father of all the gods, has an eagle perched on his scepter. His wife, Hera, keeps a peacock as her favorite pet. And his daughter, the goddess Athena, has an owl on her shoulder. Think of Hermes, the messenger of the gods. He has a winged hat, holds a winged scepter, and wears a pair of winged shoes."

"Your words have brought us much sorrow and pain," interrupted the wise old owl in a screeching voice.

"*Ah!* Our glorious past is too painful to remember," remarked Queen Nightingale with a deep sigh.

King Hoopoe nodded sadly.

"Very true. Very true." The birds' words echoed throughout the forest as they lowered their tails and heads in disappointment. They all felt disheartened and defeated.

"If only we had a way to restore our former glory and rise again," shouted an eagle from the tallest branch.

"Please, please, my feathered friends, do not despair," cried Hope, taking her chance to participate at last. She furrowed her brow, clasping her hands behind her back as she had seen her father do. Then she continued in a pensive tone. "Perhaps Trusty and I can help you become powerful again. I may have an idea," she said as she smiled and raised an eyebrow.

"Go on!" urged Trusty, looking at his friend with an eagerness to hear more. Hope hesitated for a minute, but Trusty's commanding tone filled her with courage.

"First, you need to do something daring and extraordinary," Hope advised the birds, waving a finger at the assembly. "Then, when the Olympian gods and humankind take notice, you must make your demands and somehow see them fulfilled."

Questions erupted from all sides as the birds demanded to know more.

"*Quack, quack*. How can that be?"

"*Titu, titu*. Explain yourself."

"*Cock a doodle-doooooo!* Tell us more!"

"What if you could rule the skies by building your own city, high up in the clouds?" Hope asked them, with enthusiasm. She lifted her eyes, raising both of her arms towards the sky. "You could surround your city with a tall, mighty wall and place guards at its gates. No one would enter without your permission. The Olympian gods would have to share their power with you if they still wanted to receive their precious smoke from our offerings. And we humans would have to offer you treats and sweet delicacies with honey and nuts every time we sacrifice to our gods. Otherwise . . . "

"Otherwise, we will eat your crops, poop on your white marble buildings, and let the mosquitoes bite you," interrupted the robin playfully, winking at the assembly.

Outbreaks of laughter shook the forest. The birds laughed their hearts out, flapping their wings in excitement and wagging their tails like dogs. Their sadness had dissolved into thin air!

34

"*Oop, oop, oop, upupa, upupa!* A city in the clouds!" exclaimed King Hoopoe, overwhelmed with joy. "Such a brilliant idea! Imagine! Our very own city in the clouds! Such a thing has never been attempted before. We will need an appropriate name for it . . ."

The birds began mumbling different names—Birdville . . . Bird Haven . . . Cloud-cuckoo-land . . . Cloudifornia . . . But somehow, none of them pleased the assembly, and eventually, every head turned to the wise old owl in anticipation.

Finally, after a brief period of silence, the owl hooted her wisdom. "*Who-hoo-ho-oooooo.* I believe I have the perfect name for our city." She pointed upward to the sky with one of her wings. "How about *Ornithopolis*, a bird city in the clouds?"

"*Oop, oop, oop, upupa, upupa!* That is a great name, which is worthy of our bird city," announced King Hoopoe with great satisfaction. "*Ornithopolis* it is! It will be a city like no other. We shall all live together in peace and perfect harmony, setting an example to both gods and humans alike."

"Come! Birds of a feather, work together!" ordered the king. "Fluff and preen your feathers, trim your beaks and sharpen your claws. We have a city to build. Choose the thickest cloud and let the work begin!"

Chapter Six

ROYAL ASSIGNMENTS

Happiness overwhelmed the birds, large and

small. Songs of joy filled the air. The assembly decreed that Hope and Trusty could stay in their land and help them build their city in the clouds. In gratitude, the birds presented Hope and Trusty with a magical root. It looked like a carrot, but it had purple leaves and a bitter aftertaste. The properties of *plumeradix* were a well-kept secret in the Land of the Birds. Whoever tasted this root grew temporary feathers and could fly like a bird.

Within minutes of their taking a bite of *plumeradix*, Hope's body was covered with fluffy pink feathers, like a flamingo, and Trusty grew pointed brown feathers along his arms, like an eagle. Surprised by their sudden change of appearance, the two stray dogs stood up and started barking.

While the two friends were busy admiring their feathers, King Hoopoe flew to the tallest branch and began directing the birds. He said,

"We need thirty-thousand cranes to fly to far-away lands in search of stones for our city wall.

And we need thousands of woodcocks to break down the stones into square blocks.

The storks will make mud bricks to build the walls of our buildings.

And the ducks will have to fasten their aprons and lift the bricks high up into the clouds.

The pelicans are going to bring water from the rivers and lakes to start making mud for our builders.

Geese, get ready to shovel mud with your feet into deep nests made of branches and leaves.

Eagles and hawks will grip the nests in their powerful claws and bring them to the construction site.

Hundreds of swallows will make sure that every builder has a trowel and does not run out of mud.

And finally, woodpeckers, you are our carpenters. Sharpen your beaks and get ready to chop up wood and drill holes to make doors and windows."

When King Hoopoe finished assigning a task to each bird, he dismissed the assembly, ordering all of them to get on with their work.

"Off you go, my friends. We have a city to build!"

The cranes were the first ones to take off. They picked up their portable rafts and flew off to far-away lands to bring back stones. In the meantime, the woodcocks sharpened their beaks and prepared to chip away and shape the hardest stones.

The pelicans flew to the banks of a nearby river and began kneading mud with their feet. Then the geese stepped in and used their big feet to shovel it into large nests provided by the eagles.

The storks set off to make sun-dried bricks. The pelicans assisted them by carrying water in large buckets. The ducks checked their aprons for holes, reinforcing the stitches as they lined up and waited for the bricks to dry in the hot, blazing sun.

The woodpeckers set off for the forests, and before long, a familiar drilling sound filled the air. Tall trees came crashing down, providing timber for the doors and windows of the new city. The work to build *Ornithopolis* was well underway.

Chapter Seven
SKY CLOUD CITY

In the days that followed, all birds large and small abandoned their lives on Earth and united in perfect harmony to build their Sky Cloud City. Hope and Trusty did their best to help. *Ornithopolis* started as a busy and noisy construction site, but, before long, a majestic city rose above the clouds. Tall walls with massive towers and strong gates surrounded the city.

Turkeys stood guard at the gates, ensuring that no god or human would enter the city without showing a valid traveling document. Hawks had offices next to the gates, and they were ready to stamp those documents with the official bird seal. Seagulls flew swiftly from tower to tower, overseeing the proceedings, prepared to intervene if needed.

"*Upupa, upupa, oop, oop, oop!* Our Sky Cloud City is finally complete! I am very proud of you, my friends. You may rest now and let the celebrations begin," proclaimed the king with enthusiasm.

A thick white ribbon adorned the main gate for the grand opening ceremony. As King Hoopoe lowered his crest and bent down to cut the ribbon with his beak, a messenger hummingbird darted out of nowhere. It hovered frantically in front of him, conveying a message of the utmost importance and greatest urgency.

"Your Royal Highness, King Hoopoe, ruler of *Ornithopolis* and leader of the fellowship of birds, I regret to inform you that we have a trespasser! There is an intruder among us! A goddess has sneaked into the city, without presenting her papers to the turkeys at the main gate."

A huge commotion shook the city like an earthquake! An unwelcome guest had tainted the celebrations! "Who could that be?" the question passed from mouth-to-mouth. From anger, the king's feathers turned even deeper orange . . .

It didn't take long before the intruder made her presence known to King Hoopoe. It was the feathered goddess, Iris.

"What is the meaning of all this? Why have you blocked the skies with this city?" the goddess demanded to know, taking a serious tone. "The mighty Zeus, king of the gods and ruler of humankind, sent me to find out why the people have stopped making offerings to us. It has been over a week since we last received any smoke up on Mount Olympus, and the gods are becoming restless. In the name of Zeus, I order you to explain yourselves!"

"*Oop, oop, upupa, upupa.* With all due respect, we don't need to explain ourselves, my fair goddess," replied King Hoopoe, fluffing up his feathers and opening his fanlike

crest to impress her. "From now on, we, the birds, are the rulers of the sky," he proclaimed with pride.

"You are no such thing!" shouted the goddess, pointing her staff at him in anger. "Zeus will strike you down with his thunderbolt for this insolence."

"*Ki-ki-ki!* All it takes is one word from our king, and we will fly to Mount Olympus with huge torches, and set your palaces on fire," shrieked the eagles in disdain, showing no fear. A startled goddess looked back at the eagles, suddenly realizing how powerful and determined the birds were. Her arrogance was tamed . . .

"No, my friends!" shouted King Hoopoe and flew between the eagles and the goddess, spreading his wings wide. "The fellowship of birds is wiser than this. Yes, we have the power to set their palaces ablaze, but remember that with power comes great responsibility."

Turning to the goddess, he added, "We are not looking for war, my fair goddess. You may go back to Zeus and tell him that we will restore his communication with the humans. All we ask for in return is to be treated as equals and become co-rulers of the skies, just like we used to be in the good old days."

"You are a wise and sensible ruler, King Hoopoe," replied the goddess in a softer tone. "I will present your demands to Zeus without delay." She spread her wings wide, getting ready to fly.

"Wait! Don't go yet," demanded the king. "It is my wish that you be escorted back to Mount Olympus by a dove, with a special gift for Zeus."

And turning to one of his messenger doves, he commanded, "Pick up an olive branch and offer it to Zeus with my regards—for everlasting peace and prosperity."

Chapter Eight

"ALL'S WELL THAT ENDS WELL"

The little messenger dove was received with kindness and hospitality on Mount Olympus. He was offered food and water and was allowed a day's rest before facing the mighty Zeus—ruler of the Olympian gods, god of the sky, and bearer of the thunderbolt.

When the dove appeared before Zeus, the goddess Iris spoke first. "Mighty Zeus, god of the sky, you sent me to investigate why the people have stopped sacrificing to us. Well, they haven't! The birds have built a city in the clouds. By doing so, they are blocking all the smoke that rises from the sacrifices on Earth."

Zeus frowned in anger. His voice struck them like thunder. "IS THAT SO?"

"Yes, Almighty Zeus," continued Iris. "All the birds on the planet united and worked hard until their city was complete. They have sent a dove to negotiate their terms with you."

"COME FORTH, LITTLE DOVE, AND SPEAK OUT BEFORE I LOSE MY PATIENCE," Zeus demanded.

"Powerful Zeus, bearer of the thunderbolt: King Hoopoe, the ruler of *Ornithopolis*, sends you greetings with this olive branch," spoke the dove with respect. He carefully laid the olive branch at the god's feet.

"AND WHAT DOES HE ASK IN RETURN?" Zeus wanted to know, emphasizing every word. The situation had begun to amuse him.

"With all due respect, Divine Zeus, he would like you to recognize all the birds as your equals and share the skies with them," continued the dove unafraid.

"GIVE ME ONE GOOD REASON WHY I, THE POWERFUL ZEUS, SHOULD DO THAT?"

"Because we are greater when we work together," replied the dove. He went on to remind Zeus of the birds' divine origin—and how the Olympian gods had gradually cast the birds aside.

"HM!" Zeus lifted one eyebrow and smoothed his beard with long, steady strokes. There was truth in the dove's words. This city in the skies was a major achievement, and he could not help admiring the birds for building it. *If only humans could find a way to work and live together in harmony the way the birds have done, the world would be a better place*, he thought.

After a few moments of silence, that seemed like an eternity to the little dove, Zeus spoke his mind in a kinder tone. "YOU ARE ABSOLUTELY RIGHT, LITTLE DOVE! IT IS TIME TO MAKE AMENDS AND FORGET THE MISTAKES OF THE PAST. YOU MAY RETURN TO YOUR KING AND THANK HIM FOR HIS KIND OFFERING." That said, Zeus picked up the olive branch at his feet and declared, "I WILL GLADLY SHARE THE SKIES WITH YOU AGAIN AS EQUALS, AND LET NO ONE EVER BREAK THIS NEW PACT BETWEEN US."

While this was happening on Mount Olympus, King Hoopoe sent a second messenger dove bearing an offering of goodwill to the people. The second dove's mission was to negotiate terms with humankind. It flew straight to the *Agora*, the marketplace where most people gathered every day. It perched on the large Platanus tree and began its speech.

"Greetings from his Royal Highness, King Hoopoe, ruler of *Ornithopolis*. We, the birds, have built a city high up in the sky. It blocks the smoke from your sacrifices from reaching Zeus and the Olympian gods. We are happy to correct this if you agree

to leave some offerings for us by the altars. It would be a small tribute to our services. We have served humankind well for thousands of years."

"Your offerings will keep birds from going hungry when food is scarce. Therefore, when you sacrifice to Zeus, also provide some meat for his eagles. Athena's owls have a sweet tooth, a honey-sesame bar would be a nice treat for them. Hera's peacocks adore cookies, the crows have a liking for cheese pies, and the sparrows devour sunflower seeds. And don't forget a fish or two for the seagulls."

Then the dove took out its eyeglasses, unrolled a long document, and began to read. "People, be kind, be generous, and be creative with your offerings to us. In return, we, the birds, promise to protect your homes from mice and snakes. We pledge to clear your fields from insects and worms. We agree to alert you to the change of seasons: to show you when it's time to plant your fields and to remind you when you need to prepare for winter. We, the birds, will guide your ships to port safely, and we will warn sailors when bad weather is on the way."

"As an act of goodwill, our king sends you an olive branch to seal the new pact between birds and humankind." The dove ended its speech by placing the olive branch at the base of the Platanus tree.

The people had already suffered from the birds' absence, and they were more than willing to accept the terms of the agreement. Two weeks without birds meant clouds of insects eating their crops, thousands of worms destroying their fruit, hundreds of snakes living in their fields, countless mice raiding their homes, and numerous rats running up and down their streets.

People were so impressed by what the birds had achieved that not only did they agree to their terms, but they also began imitating their ways.

It was not long before they built mechanical wings to fly and wrote music inspired by bird songs. They even paid tribute to birds by naming their children after them. Doves became symbols of peace and everlasting love. Hawks were venerated as gods, and eagles became a symbol of powerful empires.

As for Hope and Trusty, the two friends became honorary citizens of *Ornithopolis*. King Hoopoe offered them a house next to his palace, and they were free to come and go as they pleased.

Grateful as Hope and Trusty might be for this generous gift, the two friends had become homesick. The time had come for them to bid their bird friends farewell and make their way back home.

Little did they know of the new adventure that awaited them on their return to Athens—and that, my friends, is another story!

 The End

LET'S LEARN A FEW NEW WORDS . . .

Acropolis: *(noun)* an ancient fortress on a low hill in the heart of Athens. Its walls protected the city's sacred buildings.

Agora: *(noun)* the marketplace of ancient Athenians.

Almighty: *(noun)* someone with unlimited power. A title often used to describe a god or a king.

Altar: *(noun)* a marble table on which the ancient Greeks brought sacrifices to their gods and left their offerings.

Athens: *(noun)* an ancient city and the capital of modern-day Greece; named after Athena, the goddess of wisdom.

Egypt: *(noun)* a country in northern Africa; home of the Pyramids.

Eminence: *(noun)* a title often used to refer to a person of high status, such as a king or a cardinal.

Eros: *(noun)* the ancient Greek god of love. He is described as having wings and holding a bow and arrow.

India: *(noun)* a country in South Asia.

Iris: *(noun)* the ancient Greek goddess of the rainbow and a messenger of the Gods. She is described as having wings and wearing winged shoes of gold.

Nyx: *(noun)* the ancient Greek goddess of the night. Nyx was the personification of the night, and she had large, black wings.

Parthenon: *(noun)* a temple in Athens dedicated to the goddess Athena. It was built from white marble, and it still stands at the *Acropolis*—the fortified hilltop in the heart of Athens. It housed a forty-foot-high statue of Athena, made of gold and ivory.

Pendulum: *(noun)* a metal object that hangs from a fixed point and moves back and forth with the force of gravity; found in grandfather clocks.

Persia: *(noun)* an ancient country in Southwest Asia that became a vast and powerful empire.

Phoenicia: *(noun)* an ancient country in Southwest Asia at the eastern end of the Mediterranean Sea. It is the country of the Phoenicians—skillful seafarers who are considered the inventors of the alphabet.

Platanus: *(noun)* a tree that grows mostly near rivers and springs. It has leaves like those of a maple tree, and its height is between 98 and 160 feet tall.

Sacrifice: *(verb)*) to make an offering of something precious to a god or gods. For example, killing an animal on a god's altar.

Scepter: *(noun)* a decorated stick held by a king or a queen as a sign of royal authority; a staff.

Venerate: *(verb)* to worship, honor, or respect very much.

Aphrodite: goddess of love, known for her breathtaking beauty. She was born from "sea-foam," off the coast of Greece. She was married to Hephaistos, and her symbol was the dove.

Apollo: god of music, poetry and dance, truth and prophecy. Apollo was the twin brother of Artemis, son of Zeus and Leto. Exceedingly handsome and radiant like the sun, he is depicted holding his lyre and wearing a laurel wreath around his head.

Ares: god of war and the second son of Zeus and Hera. Ares was very much in love with Aphrodite. He is usually depicted wearing his armor and holding a sword and a shield.

Artemis: virgin goddess of hunting, wild nature, and childbirth. Artemis was also the protector of young girls. She was the twin sister of Apollo, daughter of Zeus and Leto. Artemis is depicted holding a bow-and-arrow, surrounded by her dogs.

Athena: virgin warrior-goddess of wisdom. She was born out of Zeus's head in full armor, with her spear, helmet, and shield. She is known as the patron goddess of Athens, and her favorite pet was the owl.

Demeter: goddess of vegetation and agriculture. Demetra was Zeus's sister. She taught humans the cultivation of wheat and the making of bread. Her symbol is a bunch of wheat.

Hephaistos: god of fire, blacksmiths, and metalworking. The first son of Zeus and Hera, he was a skillful black-smith and was married to Aphrodite. He is depicted with a beard, wearing a leather apron, and holding a hammer.

Hera: queen of both gods and humans, Hera was Zeus's sister and wife. In her marriage with Zeus, they often fought. Her favorite pet was the peacock. She is depicted holding a scepter and a pomegranate (the symbol of prosperity).

Hermes: messenger of the gods, protector of travelers and merchants, and the son of Zeus and Maia. Hermes is known for escorting the souls of dead people to the underworld, holding a feathered staff, and wearing a feathered hat and shoes.

Hestia: protector of family life, the household, and its hearth (fireplace). Hestia was Zeus's sister, and she taught humans how to build houses. Her symbol is the oil lamp.

Poseidon: god of the sea, horses, and earthquakes, and also the protector of sailors. Poseidon was Zeus's brother. His symbol is the trident. Poseidon is depicted with a long beard and holding a trident, seated on a giant seashell pulled by sea-horses.

Zeus: the supreme god in Greek mythology. As the king of both gods and humans, he demanded obedience and loyalty. He was married to his sister, Hera, and his many children included Athena, Artemis, Apollo and Hephaistos. Depicted with a long beard, he holds a scepter in one hand and a thunderbolt in the other.

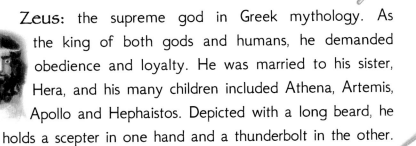

A NOTE FROM THE AUTHOR

When I was your age, I loved going to the theater. Especially in the summer, when my parents took me to plays staged in ancient open-air theaters. We sat on stone benches and, under a starry sky, watched present day adaptations of plays that were written in Athens over two thousand years ago. What a magical experience it was! One play in particular became my favorite: the comedy "The Birds" (*Ornithes*) by Aristophanes.

But who was Aristophanes? Aristophanes was born in Athens around 445 BCE and from an early age he showed a talent for writing. Before the age of twenty, he wrote his first comedy! His plays were clever, imaginative and funny. Through his work Aristophanes preached for peace, humanity and justice. Until his death, in 385 BCE, he wrote over forty comedies and received numerous awards. Unfortunately, only seven plays have survived intact.

Aristophanes' comedy "The Birds" is the story of two elderly Athenians who decided to flee the city and live with the birds! They cleverly persuaded the birds to build a fortified city in the sky. When a politician, a tax collector, a priest and a builder showed up to exploit the new city, the two Athenians sent them away. Zeus gave in to the birds' demands for equality—to avoid an unnecessary war—, and offered a beautiful goddess as a bride to one of the two Athenians!

Sky Cloud City is my retelling of "The Birds". The idea of creating a series (*The Adventures of Hope & Trusty*) inspired by Aristophanes' comedies, was born in 2013. In 2016 *Sky Cloud City* was published by Pierce Press, as a storytelling picture book. It took another five years to prepare the chapter book edition that you have just read and, hopefully, enjoyed. Hope and Trusty are ready to embark on a second—more perilous—adventure.

So stay tuned . . . !

Maria Kamoulakou-Marangoudakis is a Greek archaeologist and an award-winning children's author.

Ever since her childhood in Athens, Maria has loved escaping to the imaginary world of books. A longing to visualize and re-live the past led her to an eighteen-year career in archaeology. In 2013, a similar urge prompted Maria to test her writing abilities, and she created LITTLE CENTAUR PRESS in 2018. Her books bridge the gap between picture books and juvenile chapter books. For her themes, she searches through Greece's rich literary tradition and folklore. When not busy writing, Maria enjoys interacting with her readers at book signing events and literary festivals. She is a wildlife lover and adores traveling, meeting people, and learning about new cultures. She lives in New England with her husband, Carl, and their elderly cat, Kit-Kit.

mariakamoulakou.com • ⬛ fb.me/LittleCentaurPress

e-mail: mkamoulak@gmail.com

Natalia Kapatsoulia was born and raised in Athens, Greece.

Natalia studied French Literature at the University of Athens and Illustration at the Ornerakis School of Applied Arts. She attended illustration seminars in Italy and has participated in exhibitions in Greece, Italy, France, Japan, and Slovakia. Her career as a freelance children's book illustrator spans more than twenty years. Her favorite medium is acrylics and collage, but she also enjoys creating digital images and combining techniques. She loves drawing cute little animals in a humorous way, and her work has been shortlisted several times for the Greek state illustration awards. The book she wrote and illustrated—"Η μαμά πετάει" by Diaplasi Editions and "Mama quiere volar" by Apila Ediciones—was shortlisted for the Greek IBBY awards. Natalia currently lives and works on the island of Kefalonia with her family and her cat. She loves the sea, music, cycling, traveling, going to the movies, reading comics, and, of course, books.

nkapatsoulia.wixsite.com • ⬛ fb.me/nataliakapatsoulia

OTHER BOOKS BY THE SAME AUTHOR

littlecentaurpress.com
mariakamoulakou.com

amazon.com

amazon.com

Paperback
littlecentaurpress.com
mariakamoulakou.com
amazon.com

Hardcover
amazon.com

DON'T MISS the
FREE coloring pages
and kids' activities on
mariakamoulakou.com

Manufactured by Amazon.ca
Bolton, ON

27077394R00036